DO YOU BELIEVE IN THE HEREAFTER?

DO YOU BELIEVE IN THE HEREAFTER?

Book III

TINA WYATT

Do You Believe in the Hereafter?
Copyright © 2019 by Tina Wyatt. All rights reserved.

No part of this publication may be reproduced, stored in a retrieval system or transmitted in any way by any means, electronic, mechanical, photocopy, recording or otherwise without the prior permission of the author except as provided by USA copyright law.

This novel is a work of fiction. Names, descriptions, entities, and incidents included in the story are products of the author's imagination. Any resemblance to actual persons, events, and entities is entirely coincidental.

The opinions expressed by the author are not necessarily those of URLink Publishing.

1603 Capitol Ave., Suite 310 Cheyenne, Wyoming USA 82001
1-888-980-6523 | admin@urlinkpublishing.com

URLink Publishing is committed to excellence in the publishing industry.

Book design copyright © 2019 by URLink Publishing. All rights reserved.

Published in the United States of America
ISBN 978-1-64367-692-0 (Paperback)
ISBN 978-1-64367-691-3 (Digital)

01.08.19

I wrote this book as a follow-up to my second one.
A lot of people asked me to write it, so I
hope everyone enjoys reading it.
This is from my heart to you.
Tina Wyatt.

To pick up where I left off in my second book, a lot of people have asked me to write another book. so here goes book 3. I hope you all enjoy it.

I do have more stories to share with you. I still have things flare up from the truck accident over several years ago. Some things that I just love to live with. But I am a fighter. I was in the hospital trying to pass three kidney stones. I was in my room by myself. Had got up to go to the bathroom, took George with me. I call that IV Packor, that pack you are hooked up to you take with you, Hahaha. But when He left the room, it started dumping all those towels in sink. When one afternoon I was lying in bed watching TV, wishing I could go home, Bud had left to go home, I was just watching TV, cooking, there was a chair over by the door, when all of a sudden it was just like someone sitting in that chair. I thought I was seeing things. It happened again. A nurse came in I told her what had happened. She said "well, you said your kid came to visit sometime. They all know about my books, some of them have them.

Now a story about my healing, the power of god. I had a knot in my upper part of my stomach, it hurt bad. They said it was a blockage in my upper bowels. This place was a large lump that went across my stomach. One afternoon, I had prayed to God for a healing. He told me to sing a religious song, it came to me to sing to the garden. All of a sudden, on the last verse, and he walks with me, and talks with me, and He tells me, I am His own. I hold my hand on my stomach, all of a sudden, I felt a jerk, it was gone. I call the nurse in to check me she said "where did it go? What happened?" I said "God took it away". They ran a scan a CT scan on me, it was gone. I told them I just did what God told me to do. Thank you, Jesus, I was hurting so bad. Ask and believe, he can heal you to.

Last time I was in the hospital, I was put on blood thinners, I hate it, but I have to be on them for the last six months. And it took two visits to the E.R. to find out what was going on. I hate to get a Doctor that does not now you. Here, people call them rent-a-Doctor. I wish I could still have the old-fashioned Doctor. Instead of going to different Doctors for things one Doctor could have took care off for you. Grew up with only one family Doctor, but that was the good old days. And a family Doctor knew what was going on with you. I just do not think to get one of those Doctor just won't to run all kinds of test on you. If you have good insurance you will get care.

I was prepared for surgery twice. A Doctor could not figure out what anesthesia he could use. So far, two weeks in the hospital on a lot of medication I did not need. I passed two kidney stones at the hospital and one at home and had to take a lot of medication I did not need to take.

Now some stories from the afterlife world, people have shared with me. My husband had a guy helping at our woodshop T&B Woodworks. This guy said he turned and he saw someone standing beside him from the corner of his eye. Said he turned to see what he wanted and he was not there. He was telling me about it, he was describing what the man looked like. I showed him the picture on the back of my book, he said that it's him. I told him my son came home to help us run the shop. He loved being at the shop. I think He knew He was going to die as I look ack on it now. He paid his rent two months ahead of time and bills – electric, water, etc. I think He know He was going to pass away. But I did not want to face it. Either it's been eight years now, I still miss Him every day.

But my son still loves to fester me. When He was alive, he loved to bug me. I was cleaning out my fridge getting ready for the Christmas, making room for food. I had been having trouble with it. Blood pressure being low, I was getting light headed a lot, then that night I had just went to bed. I started dreaming. Here comes my son in my dream.

We had just moved in a beach house. He had brought a lot of kids home from school. Bud had brought a little black dog home. He was afraid it might get run over in parking lot. It was a puppy about two months old. So Wess and his friends was playing in the house. They were singing. One kid said "Wess, you should make a CD, you are a good singer" I come in, asked where is little puppy, one kid said "do it Wess, let it out" when we came in. I told Wess, "you better go find it! It's just a baby" so he goes looking for it. "You better go find it!"

LITTLE LOST DOG

So, there he is walking around, singing. "oh where, oh where, can that damn little dog be, he ran away and I don't give a damn" he said. I asked "what did you say?" He said "I do not have time to look for that darn dog! I want to play with my friends!" I said, "well, I wonder if you want or like a good ass whipping, I am going to give to you" well, I got my blood pressure up. I woke up looking for Him.

My kids were taught respect for us. And I did not put up with kids talking back to me. But where they got a spanking, it was on the butt.

SOME HAIR CARE PRODUCTS

About those hair care products that say can get your hair back, I used on for seven days, I was desperate to get my hair back. So, I heard about a product said, guaranty to get hair back. All it did to me was cause those big cysts. After I got out of the hospital, I called them, asked me to send it back to them and they would refund my money, I did not do it. I thought about it. If I did, I would now see money again.

I just hope they find all those people missing in that hurricane that had 150 miles and has winds that hit land. I saw on Facebook three little kids were missing. I pray they find them just Babies. Some of the people I saw is terrified said next time a hurricane is coming and they are told to 12. Some of them did not thank it was going to be that bad.

A DREAM FROM A FRIEND

More of Hereafter. My daughter told me about a dream she has had a few times. It is about a friend of all of Owens. He died of course. His wife has remarried said, she married a guy that has beat up his ex-wives and girlfriends. And has gotten everything. This guy left for his son from money to an old truck his daddy loved and waited soon loved it. This guy always waited the best for his family. She, my daughter said He comes to her in dreams last one he said "please, please, help her I told".

MY DAUGHTERS DREAM

You are getting a message from the spirit world. I ask her "what did you say to him?" She said "I am sorry but she does not want to be around us anymore". I told her I just bet he does not understand that because when he was alive you all were so close. I told her I know he watches over them. And she asks me what should she do? I said "just tell him she does not want you all in her life anymore. My daughter said "it is so sad". And he has showed up in her dreams two times.

MORE STORIES FROM SPIRIT WORLD.

For a week I had this dream over and over. This little boy came to me and he said "some boys put Him in a cave and he could not get out. He was dressed in older clothes, a striped T-shirt and tore up jeans. He was really dirty. He was about five years old. I told my niece Sandy about my dream she said "let me help you." She had a dream she saw a little boy who told him to go to the light. It was strange, after that I stopped having that dream.

I believe your pets can come back in spirits too. My dog Junior. He was 14 years old he had not been real sick. Bit after his 14th birthday he got really sick. I took his to the vet. He was getting medication for two weeks. So, one weekend he got really bad. We took him to a vet not the one we were taking him to for years. We had just left him with vet. She called two hours later and said he died.

Buds sister was blind but she said "I always had lots of Dogs around me." When she was in the hospital just before she died, we went to visit her. She said my dogs were trying to get her food so I just told my dogs "come on, let's go." She said she could see them all around me. Now remember she was blind I sure do miss her. She was like a sister to me. But she does visit me in my dreams sometimes.

Remember the house next door I told you about? Well, people still do not live there for very long. One of our neighbors lives on the other side of it. She said every time she walks by it; she feels strange. I told her the preacher across the street has blessed it. I just home the guy in football suit has gone to the other side. The owner of that has redone kitchen, floors and went up on rents. And has put up a new fence up. It is a nice place.

TORNADO WHEN I WAS A KID.

But like I said people just do not live there for very long. It has a storm cellar, a dirty one. I know I was in it with a family when all those tornados came through Pampa, Texas. Those people had stuff stored in it. We were all standing in water almost up to over knees. I was glad when It was over. I came back to my house. My doors would keep on opening it was so strange like I was in a twilight zone. When I was a kid we lived in Oklahoma and took our bath in Red River.

I was four years old when a tornado got our house. I remember seeing a big black cloud, my sister ran in and told my momma. Mama said everyone get to cellar, my grandpa Abe said he was not going, it would blow over.

Momma said your stupid sob; it is coming right for us. She said "kids get in circle". Grandpa decided he would go to. After he looked out and saw it was coming across the corn field. She was flying over where it was so scary momma would not let us come out of the cellar.

But I remember seeing things flying around her and grandpa was holding door I remember saying "God please save us". After tornado got our house momma got a mattress and quilts but I remember water in cellar, I thought we were going to drown.

Next day when we got out of the cellar, a tree was in our house, clothes was in trees. Momma had been churning butter milk my sister and I had been begging for the butter that was coming out the top of the churn wall it was on top of bed all poured out. Everything in house was gone out thing were scattered all over. Daddy was across the river he said "It had rose up from all the rain from the storm." But he swam across it to get home. Momma was crying when he came home. But I remember daddy saying "things can be replaced but not lives". We were all glad to be together again.

Daddy came up with a big old tent we lived in for a while. It had dirty floors but momma made a home for us. When we moved in to another house. Grandpa lived in the tent outside of our house. And daddy got some big pigs them darn things would chase my sister and I, every time we were playing outside. We were so afraid of them. But they were our food along with other food daddy brought home.

And we had a garden, got fresh vegetable. My Daddy had a green thumb, he could grow big vegies and water melon and cantaloupes. Will now it be time for my brother had to come along. Grandmother was there and aunt Elsa.

I was 6 years old my aunt Elsa got this ideal for us my sister and I to watch the birth of my brother. She had us watching looking through a window momma was hurting so bad. She was screaming we were crying trying to get to her. My grandmother told aunt Elsa "you are going to get a whipping after your sister has this baby." I remember that old doctor just standing in front of a mirror messing with his mustache. He said it is coming along fine. I did not see him doing anything. Momma was having my brother with no medication. She made it. He was born. My grandma brought us in to see him he was in a blanket she took it off of him. We were standing there looking at our little brother, we were looking him over. He started peeling on us Memaw said "oh my gadget, a diaper on him". Everyone was laughing about that he hot us right in the face.

There was six of us, three of my brothers were born in the hospital. My grandmother said "all daddy had to do was having his paints on momma's bed and she got pregnant. My grandmother had a way with words. I miss her so much. But I have seen

DAUGHTERS DREAM

Here in my dreams I always had lots of fun when I got to visit her in summer time she taught me lot of things. How to make crafts. She taught me how to make nanny toaster cover. I made a lot of them while Bud was in the Navy. But I did run on to one guy would not let his wife have one. He said it reminded him of his grandmother's love. I said "I like all color of people. And It is just called a nanny doll toaster cover.

Red and Yellow, Black or White. We are all precious in his sight. And we are all brothers and sisters in God's eyes. My Memaw taught me you treat people right. They will do the same for you.

Now a hobby I have picked up collecting old coins. My daddy found one of the 1945 copper penny's in an old purse. He found at a dump. He had it marked with red nail polish, had it in his overalls pocket. Forgot to take it out of his pocket. Lost it at a Borger TX Laundry. Matt went back and ask them if they found it. Said they did not find it. That coin is worth thousands so I still check my penny's. In hopes if my finding daddy's penny again. He was so proud of it. And I told him I hope you remember to take your penny out of little pocket before you wash your overalls, he said he did. He was so sad he told me "would you believe I lost that damn penny. I also went to laundry Matt and ask them about it." Just told daddy lost some change in one of their washers. It would really be something if it was still in that washing machine or a drain. I am also looking for a three-legged buffalo nickel worth a lot of money. My brother sold a dime for $300.00 one time. Just old coins. I saw a guy on Facebook found a lot of coins in a picture frame. They were opening it up with a crow bar, a coin collecting all looked very new. Then I saw this little boy with a hammer hitting them. It made me sick I wrote them a message, I told them, "Your coins will not be worth much all beat up." But some kids just go spend them and do not know what old coins are worth.

COIN COLLECTION GONE

Had has in one of those old churches that fold out in to a bed. But after she passed away there was not much left of her coin collection. I told everyone you do not realize how much some of those coins were worth.

But something happened with my son and daughter in law. Her mom and dad had a big coin collection. And my son said "mom we need food more than we need that coin collection". And I did not have the money to buy it from him or them. But when were at grocery store, my daughter in law and I were at grocery store. I was paying for food for supper. I went over three dollars. I started to put something back. My daughter in law said "hey mom, let me pay for it" that cashiers' eyes light up. She told her I will give you three dollars each for all those quarters. This made me sic to see this

But my son got his favorite meal. Pancit, lumpia apricot sauce. When we came home, I told my son "if you are going to sell those coins, you need to find a coin collector Bud. Some of them are worth a lot of money". He said "momma like I said, I have to feed my family". We help them as much as we could. He had just started his weed spraying company. Was not making much. We also helped him with that. And sometimes we waited to get paid waiting on people to pay him for jobs. I told him "son, get paid or at least half before you agree to do a job for them". He finally got it all together, and we had more jobs then we could handle. But we had over arguments. But got over them. We still loved each other. But did find out not a good ideal working for kids. Sometimes he would come around and check on us to see if we were doing our job. I got mad one day and said "get your fat ass out and help us". We had done three yards, that day was so tired. He said "mom I am sorry you are fired". I said "fine, I am going home". Bud stayed with him for a while until he could find someone else. He did one guy sprayed some flowers at a car lot here at Pampa, TX. It wound up to my son. Could not get good help so he got his wife Jan. They came by our house just before Wess got a hold of head hunters for a job. Jan looked like a blue smurf.

 I told her "you had to get in a shower not good to be breathing that weed spray". I ask her "how did that happen?" she said "I was mixing the dye with dish soap when tank filled up fast and pressure hit her in the face". I could not keep from laughing at her, I said "I am sorry, but you look like a blue smurf. She said "I know and I am pissed off" he said "Wess was yelling at her and she was not watching what she was doing". But after that, Wess got jobs at different meat packing plant. And yes, made good money like $80,000 a year. So, when they came home for a visit, we all had fun but I worried about him. His weight was 440 lbs. Thus, close to 300, you all know he passed away 8 years ago and lost time. I saw her. She had lost a lot of weight. He got fired because on his weight on April fool's day he calls us I could not believe it; thought he was pulling an April fool's joke when he called us. He said "they said he was just on a try out for a while, anyway said he was too big to climbing on them ladders. But did not matter". He made them a lot of money and he was working on a pipe where they pump meat to be chopped up. They dumped a lot of meat in with him, he said he was covered in meat. The only way he got out was a hose he climbed up to ger out of it. He said he thought he was going to die that day. But he came home and died from a staph infection from a burn he got at the plant at Washington State. He was welding something and a piece of hot metal went through his glove got a burn on his hand. He came home his hand was twice its size. He went in the hospital, they let him out, was not over staph infection. I thank the insurance ran out, he had to go back two weeks later to cut his arm off. Then decided to try antibiotic again. We took him back. He was having trouble seeing. He went in hospital again. But some of them just acted like that fat man is here again. But each time they sent him home the insurance had run out. To me it is sad when it depends on how much insurance you have to get good care.

    I look back on it now and I thank my Son was not going to live much longer. And he knew. It was like he was getting prepared. And he had that for away, look in his beautiful eyes. I just wish I could have done more to help him. I know his spirit does visit us. One time, I saw him in my bathroom, I was coming to bed. I looked in the bathroom saw him standing in front of mirror. I first thought it was Bud my husband.

HERE AFTER

I came to bed. Walked in bedroom. Bud was in bed. I had chill go over me so I went back and checked the bathroom again and no one was there. He looked young and healthy but he was looking in that mirror. I see him more in my dreams and if something is going on in our family, I see him more. When I see him, it is just like a flash, I wish I could talk to him sometimes. And I have seen flashes of my family and friends. But I can talk to them in my dreams but I can feel their presence when they came around. Sometimes I smell my best friends' perfume so I knew she has come to visit me. And I have smelled a shaving cologne in a room. A friend of mine named Fannie said that is a visit from someone from the afterlife. And sometimes a warning, something is going to happen to someone you know. She asks me "what was the smell of it?" I said "old spice". She was visiting us and she said she needs to call home. She found out her father in law was in hospital really sick. And yes, he wore old spice cologne. My friend was a believer a lot of from the islands are believers in the afterlife. I keep on watching for Kilauea to stop erupting. The legend goes, when you see a hand with five fingers volcano is supposed to stop erupting.

Hey folks I got my cookbook published. It is called Welcome to Tina's Kitchen; Lets cook together. I am very proud of it. It has my recipes, my mamas' friends and recipe from overseas. Hawaii, Guam, Philippines, Germany; I forgot a very important person, my grandmother. She made some great food and homemade. I loved her Banana pudding, chicken and dressing the old fashioned one and she put boiled eggs chopped up in it. I know I'm making everyone hungry, me too. I miss their food so much. But the main reason I wrote my cookbook is because when I am fixing one of the recipes my husband Bud would say "are you sure you put that in the recipe?" I just get my cookbook and say "right there it is.

Now, do not get me wrong he can cook good food too. He fixed us hamburger stew last night. It was so good to me a soup it is the spot once cold and rainy day and yes, he cooked it in a pressure cooker.

I have been watching a program on TV. People looking for their loved ones. Babies that they gave away out of bad luck. I have had people say no you cannot keep your baby. I do not understand that, that baby did not ask to come in this world. And some grandparents forget that, that baby is their grandchild. The show I was watching last night. Baby was left in a shoe box at a service station, mother was a young woman with four other kids to raise. Mother lost her husband with a heart attack. Mother was having a hard time taking care of other kids after the husband passed away but back then they did not have food stamps or places people could get help. Mother said she watched to make sure someone picked up shoe box with baby in it then she said she went home and cried. Well, these people who found her did a DNA test. She found her mother, she was 93 years old. I cried with them when she met her mother after those years. Her mother explained to her what happened. And she had thought about her for years. And her mother said "I did not know if you would even forgive me" daughter said she was raised by great family that love her but there was just an emptiness not knowing what her story was. Did not want to thank her mother did not love her she just needed to

DAUGHTER FINDS MOTHER

Her story she went back and sit down where she was left at that service station was mother anymore so she sat down on side walk and said "that is where her life began", then you see the walk through the door to meet her mother. I was crying with them, it all turned out great. Her mother was in a chair said "I am sorry I cannot get up and hug you. Daughter said "don't you worry I will take care of you and I have a hugs, loved you mama. If we had all the programs we have now, people would not be giving their babies away. We had two kids a boy and a girl. I done with food to feel them one time and I love them so much. I would die for them. We lost our son six years ago. He passed in his sleep. But you all know him as Wesley. I talk a lot about him in my books. My daughter's name, we call her sis or Monkey Kat sometimes, lol.

    She comes to visit us and I talk to her every day. We have lots of fun when she visits us. But right now, she has a lot to deal with her sickness with IBS and husband just had surgery. He had a melanoma and was cancer but they said got it. He is still having complications since he has had surgery. I hurt for him and I pray he gets well. He is a very sweet person. I always told my daughter he was God sent to us. We all have treated daughter in law Jan and son in law like our kids.

DO YOU BELIEVE IN THE HEREAFTER?

I am lying here in my bed watching TV and writing my fourth book. I just looked; I have showed this to other people I have a stuffed toy on a shelf. It says gone Bananas my sons face shows up to me sometimes. I have showed it to other people. Some of them could see and some could not. But I have tried to get a picture of it. It just shows up Gone Banana's. I can also see colors around people sometimes.

It hurts you bad when it is family and you give them stuff to help them. Then you find out they gave it away or sell it at a pawn shop. When you give it to them, they acted like they really wanted it. Then you hear, they gave it away or sold it. Some of their things I gave away were new. I got it just paying shipping and handling so I thought I was helping, giving my grandkids things. I had two still in the box.

MOTHER IN LAW TROUBLE.

But I was not treated like family for a while so I know how it feels. It took a lot of years for my husbands' mom to accept me until one day it all came to an end. She was saying how good her son was, taking care of us, and she was visiting with us, just before we got the flood at North Carolina. I was so mad at Bud; we had not heard from him. All I knew was a Hurricane was hitting New Orleans. And he was on a ship and she was bragging on him what a great family man he was. I was not supposed to say anything about her baby boy. I got so mad and her have it. I said "sure, he is a family man but right now he does not care what we are going through." I was so pissed off. I was crying, I did not hear from him until we moved in trailer house at Charleston, SC. She went home before the flood. But ever since out blow up she treated me like a daughter. Everyone in family said I should have done it sooner but I did not want to hurt their feelings. She loved my cooking though when we came home on leave, she would have me make her some of it. She could make great desserts. But not so good with everyday meals. But Buds dad did most of the cooking. And after she passed away, he lived with us. He was called dad-dad. I was at work he fixed a pot of beans forgot he put salt in them two times. I put a potato with skin in pot but still could not get salt taste out. But he was just trying to help me having a meal fixed when I got home, he loved to cook and he always cooked a big turkey for everyone for Christmas, in a big old roaster cooker and I hated to clean it. Now are you ready for more from the spirit world. Here goes. I have an adjustable bed, I had to jump up get to bathroom fast. I put the control at the end of my bed. My bed was up to where I could be up in my bed with a pillow behind my back, I come back to my bed. My bed was completely down, Bud was asleep and I left. On the foot of my bed with remote control and phone. I just said "Wess, cut it out". He loves to beg me, sometimes I can almost hear him laughing at me when I saw my bed flat down. I told him "Stop it. I know you did it. You have to push that button before the bed will raise up." He messes with my touch lamp too. Yesterday I was eating mango, I had it on a tray on my bed, I was cutting its skin off when he turned the light off. He loved to pester me when he was alive so now, he does from afterlife. And sometimes I see a showdown on wall in hallway right now I see an outline of a push on hall wall and his picture is in hall at night I can see a light shining on his picture. I will try and get a picture of it. And put it in this book. Sometimes I will be sleeping. And feel something touching my hair when I am asleep. I check it is not Bud, my son always loved to mess with my hair.

EXPERIENCE AT FUNERAL

My daughter said when she is at a funeral. She has felt someone pulling her hair. And her people have seen this happen to her. She had really long hair one time she had it in a long braid said she was standing there and someone was pulling on her hair. I just told her someone was trying to communicate with you from the other side. She said "mom, it is scary" so she got to where she would wear her hair up and she said it still happens when she is at a school yard.

To run our country not people that are causing trouble all the time back stabbing. I pray Republicans and Democrats get all this straighten out. That is what our enemy's want. We are a great country but if people do not wake up, we could lose it. But got has got to where you cannot turn on your tv. Someone is making fun of our president. Sad that our country has got like every night a talk show comes on. I can remember when it was fun to watch but this one comes on late night. Last night they started out making fun of president Trump. I just cannot understand how these people are getting away with this. In the past you would be put in jail for some of the thing people are doing and saying or I will get down of my soap box before I forget I told you all about that lady at Florida. Everyone was saying she was in the house that got destroyed in hurricane Michael. They found her and She said she plans on rebuilding her home. She had to have taken a ride like Dorothy in Wizard of OZ. Now for some more of Do you believe in the hereafter, last time we were people from Dr. Office. At Dr. Office we all got to talking. I met a lot of people that told me they have got visits from family and friends. Once lady saw us in parking lot said she usually hates to wait in waiting room to see Doctor but she really had a good time talking with us. Everyone has things happen that they do not understand. What they have seen or a dream of loved one; myself and I thank that how our.

But it hurts you, when you think you helped someone only to get hurt. And some friend that say they are your friend and find out they are just talking about you to other people behind your back and you find out about it. It hurts. I know some of the people I know say things and her witch hazel, I do not care, it is real to me. And I have asking "Doctor, is there anything wrong? Health wise, that is causing me to see things other people cannot see?" he said I have been told that it is a gift from God. I had a hard time believing when it first started happening with me. But now I know I am not the only one this happens to. And I can tell when I meet a person that does not believe or want to get one of my books and that is ok. Bud, I am so happy when I hear you helped me through a bad time. When I lost a loved one or a friend. I feel I helped that person and I feel great about it. It is a wonderful feeling family and friends communicate with us. I meet so many people now that tells me they believe in the afterlife when they find out I write books they started telling me about a visit so you hear a noise in the night it could be a visit for you from the hereafter so enjoy it, I do. And the color I chose for this book is for family and friends

you need it. Don't get me wrong. I was in a nursing home two and a half months after the truck accident. I met a lot of nice people but I also had rounds with some of the people that worked there about patients. It is just not right to treat a person like a kid when they still have a mind and know what is going on with them. It was sad to see, I was in. Once a doctor said I could not stay at home. It is when you first go in one. I did not know at that time when and if I would ever get out. Bud was with me every day. I also had them bring a tray of food the insurance was paying for it. He was always bringing fruits and candy for me and all the nurses they all loved him. One of the patients got a crush on him I told her "lady, you are a sweet person but he is my man. You need to leave him alone." Hes buying you coffee in a morning cooking meal for you. Last night I have slept almost all afternoon. I am trying to get use to a medication that has side effects Eliquis it is a blood thinner. They did test said I had blood, lots in my legs and lungs. And I have to take this blood thinner for six months. So ladies, you get you a good man like I have hold on to him, I love when she still ask him to come to her room before we left. I told him she better not kisses you. He said he just hugged her and said goodbye. She would always be out at the place they had to smoke cigarettes and Bud said she got cigarettes off him. I said "she loved you for your cigarettes." He said he was big fat and ugly that is what he always says when someone ask him how do you feel today. He always says that.

Says you are beautiful to me. I see an old lady in my mirror; grey hair and wrinkles. But I still love for him to say that. But we are both recycled teenagers. What we use to, does fun now. It is work lol. You know laughing out loud. But since my last surgery when I had those cysts as big as tennis balls on my butt and I got sepsis over it. People please watch the Hair Stuff. If I did send it back, I would not hear from them. And was it going to get back my hair. What I want through it. I also had to have home care service thank God. Those nurses helped me cleaned my wounds, took care of me. I love the mall; I had a choice washing home or I said home care. I got them to take care of me for seven years off and on. It helps me to have good insurance that pages for you to get good care

I told Bud "you do not know anymore when women are flirting with you or maybe he does sometimes" he says things to people that makes them smile especially women. I have seen this or tell someone a joke they say "Oh, you made my day". But people say I can do that to you, treat people right, they will do the same for you. Now I have met people out of my life. I have helped people. Food and I know a lot of people do not believe but this was real to me. I thought for a long time. I am the only one this has happened to. Now I hear more people talking about what they saw. We now have Doctors. A lot of people that have had after death thing that happened to them when they went to heaven and was sent back. My mother always said "When it's your time there is nothing you can do about it."

I told you all about my after-life experience when my son was born in 1963 Dec 17th. And one more thing I will share. Jesus had place on his wrist not his hands. He looked like the man in my book with a crown of thorns but did not have them in his head. Just a glow it was beautiful. It was a feeling I will never forget my visit in heaven with Jesus.

I do not know I told you all. Sometimes I have dreams about people. I had one last night. I needed to tell my daughter about. I think we can get a message from a friend or family from the afterlife. A good friend was in the dream that died from cancer. The message was one of my daughters' dogs was going to be sick and to check her old coins for an old coin that could be worth a lot of money out for Cassie and check her change.

I need to share this, it happened. I had just told my daughter about wind chime in my front room door way, someone moved it. I just had it ding. I have a cleaning service someone moved it to dust around door seal. I saw it hanging on wall on my left the bell sound. This may sound strange to you but I am worth dying if my son does not like it that someone moved it. In dreams, she was going to use it for a garage sale, some coins are worth thousands. Will folks, did you hear in India? People are putting the mark of the beast on babies foreheads. But we all have a number in the United States. It is called Social Security. We all have one. And if you do not have a green card and think you can live here. You are called Illegal Alien and did you even think we would be hearing a president of USA

In Buds family, they have a superstitious; you do not give a crap I got that wrong. A woman does not give another woman one rose. It is bad luck. I did not know it is bad. Got med rose. Well it looked like one of you pull it. It was a pair of red panties. I got Peg one for a love she said "Tina, please don't give that to me" and I got her a yellow one. She said "I am not ready to die.

Years after his wife and her husband passed away. One of those loves that never die Ken was with Peg when she passed away. He told me we just found each other after 30 years. Ken was Pegs first love. I think we all have a first love we never forget. But when you find your soulmate that is the one you are happy with and send those golden years together. Loving each other being there after you are sick mind.

I just thought it would be funny. But I think she lived five years after that she was so much fun and a sister to me. She raised three kids and was blind but could cook, dance and nothing could stop her. But I do wonder she is in heaven she loved two men. Her first husband she lost at 39 years old and her second husband Ken she loved him first he was her mommas and dads tv repair man they got back together.

People on tv, making fun of him you cannot turn on your tv anymore. You do not see someone making fun of him. People, he is the leader of our Country he was voted in to be the President of the United States. And at least he has done things other presidents have not. I also heard them trying to drag first lady down asking her stupid questions about her husband.

I just cannot remember in the past. Where only of our past president were treated like this one. But I will say this for our first lady she stood up to reporters said "you cannot believe everything you hear on the news, some of it is called fake news. So do not believe everything you hear. It is sad that our country has like this. We need good leaders for

Now I am going to talk about something else. I am glad to hear women are talking about being sexually abused. I have been put in a closet long enough. I was watching Dr. Oz today about a doctor examining women without gloves on and had them take of their clothes in front of him, three hundred women. Brought back a memory to me just before I had my gallbladder surgery I had to go to several times before the Dr. Decided I needed my gallbladder took out. This happened at a pearl harbor ER. I was in so much pain. It was making me sick. I was laying there on table or hard bed waiting on doctor to come in to check me. I just had a gown on, you know those see more butts' ones. I was in so much pain he started rubbing his penis against my leg with erection. I look at him and said "what in the world do you think you are doing? I want my husband in here" he said "you just need to be still. And let me check you" I said No you sob you need to get me another doctor then I screamed for Bud, he came in. Said what is wrong with you doctor. Said she will not let me check her I said no I will not tell him what you did he said I was just trying to check you, out. I said not with your penis on my leg. He said he did not do that I said you are a lying sob. next thing I know he took out of there. Three other doctors in came. And asked me what was going on I told them what happened. They told me don't worry about him he will be gone and we are sorry that happened to you. I just wonder how many other women he did that to and they never said anything about it. I did and glad I did. The way he was smiling. I think he would have raped me if he thought I would let him. This was years back before a nurse had to be in room with you when doctor examined you. I am glad they do now have a nurse in the room with when a doctor checks you over. Because you never know when you are going to get horny doctor. The rest of my story did have my gallbladder took out. It was closing up. Was not working right. I spent two weeks in hospital. Got 18 stiches out of it. I was away from my kids. Bud brought them to my window in my room. They were too young to be on the floor where I was at. They were crying and wanted to hug me. Nurse came in and said you are not supposed to be out of bed. I said you leave me alone. I am looking at my babies. I have not seen them in two weeks because of your rules.

Now for a story I just remembered. My cousins house caught on fire a year ago. House was caught with fire. All on one wall there was a picture of Jesus you could see where fire got everything on walls except the picture Jesus. I just saw this happened in news this what someone said and showed picture on wall from hurricane Michael at Florida. God bless all those people and I have all of our pictures in hallway but at night. I can look down the hallway there is a light shining on his picture I know this sounds strange to some people but I can see it in the dark. I will try and get a picture of it so you all can see it too. I know I have seen a lot of things other people cannot see. But this has happened to me since 1963 when I was holding Jesus hand

What I have seen on the looks like a bomb has it those people at Florida. I was watching a news reporter on tv when hurricane Michael hit. She was in a hotel looking out a window reporting the news. There was a big blue house across street next thing we all look over blue house is gone. They said was a lady in it ridding out storm. I hope they found her but that house was gone. All you see the land it was sitting on. I will never forget seeing that.

www.ingramcontent.com/pod-product-compliance
Ingram Content Group UK Ltd.
Pitfield, Milton Keynes, MK11 3LW, UK
UKHW022217230426
12048UKWH00016BA/903